By Joan Walsh Anglund

A FRIEND IS SOMEONE WHO LIKES YOU
THE BRAVE COWBOY
LOOK OUT THE WINDOW
LOVE IS A SPECIAL WAY OF FEELING
IN A PUMPKIN SHELL
COWBOY AND HIS FRIEND
CHRISTMAS IS A TIME OF GIVING
NIBBLE NIBBLE MOUSEKIN
SPRING IS A NEW BEGINNING
COWBOY'S SECRET LIFE
A POCKETFUL OF PROVERBS
CHILDHOOD IS A TIME OF INNOCENCE
A BOOK OF GOOD TIDINGS
WHAT COLOR IS LOVE?
A YEAR IS ROUND
A IS FOR ALWAYS
MORNING IS A LITTLE CHILD
DO YOU LOVE SOMEONE?
THE COWBOY'S CHRISTMAS
A CHILD'S BOOK OF OLD NURSERY RHYMES
A BIRTHDAY BOOK
THE CHRISTMAS COOKIE BOOK
THE JOAN WALSH ANGLUND STORYBOOK
EMILY AND ADAM

For Adults

A CUP OF SUN
A SLICE OF SNOW
GOODBYE, YESTERDAY
ALMOST A RAINBOW
THE CIRCLE OF THE SPIRIT

A·CHRISTMAS·BOOK

JOAN
WALSH·ANGLUND

RANDOM HOUSE   NEW YORK

For Emily's new brother, Thaddeus,
on his first Christmas

Copyright © 1981, 1983 by Joan Walsh Anglund.
All rights reserved under International and Pan-American Copyright Conventions.
Published in the United States by Random House, Inc., New York, and
simultaneously in Canada by Random House of Canada Limited, Toronto.

Library of Congress Cataloging in Publication Data:
Anglund, Joan Walsh. A Christmas book.
SUMMARY: A collection of stories and poems, with a play, for Christmas.
1. Christmas—Literary collections. [1. Christmas—Literary collections] I. Title.
PZ7.A586Ci 1983 [E] 83-3384 ISBN: 0-394-85551-5 (trade); 0-394-95551-X (lib. bdg.)
Manufactured in the United States of America 2 3 4 5 6 7 8 9 0

A
TABLE OF
CONTENTS

SWEET CHRISTMAS

It's Christmas! Sweet Christmas!
the glad bells tell the news
It is the day . . . the childhood day,
of Joy we never lose

It's Christmas! Sweet Christmas!
        The Happy day of Home.
Let's trim the tree . . . and give our gifts,
        And then together come

Together . . . together
        Let's say the silent prayer
Of "Peace on Earth
        Good Will to Man"
For All men . . . Everywhere!

THE BIG DOLL AND THE TEDDY BEAR

Once, many years ago, there was a big porcelain doll and a brown teddy bear who sat side by side on a shelf in a small toy store.

They had been sitting side by side on that same high, dark shelf for several years now... ever since they'd been mistakenly tucked away up there by a new clerk. The shelf was much too high for anyone to reach easily, and so, of course, all the other toys on the lower shelves were chosen one by one and taken from the store to go and live in the homes of children. But month after month the big porcelain doll and the brown teddy bear just sat there, side by side, gathering dust.

As they looked down from their high shelf, they could see all the people shopping down below. My, how busy it seemed to be lately! Much busier than it had ever been before.

"What could be happening down there?" asked the porcelain doll.

"I don't know," answered the teddy bear, "but whatever it is, it must be something special!"

And, indeed, it *was* something special. Christmas was coming! In fact, it was Christmas Eve, and all the people were in a flurry to buy their last-minute gifts before the stores closed. Hour after hour the doll and the teddy watched people come into the shop and buy all the different toys from the lower shelves. One little boy bought a drum for his cousin. A girl in a red coat admired a tea set, and after she left the store, her aunt came back and purchased the prettiest tea set of all. A busy father hurried in with a long list and ordered some toy soldiers, a sailboat, a train set, a yellow duck, and a jack-in-the-box.

Customer after customer opened the shop door and left again, carrying away toy after toy. But *no* one, of all the many customers that night, ever even glanced up at the higher shelf. No one asked, even once, for the big porcelain doll or her friend, the brown teddy bear.

"Where do all the toys go after they've

11

been wrapped up and taken away?" asked the doll wistfully. "What would it be like to be some little girl's favorite doll? I guess no one will ever buy us, so I don't suppose I'll ever know!"

"Neither will I," said the bear. "I always thought *I* would belong to some little boy. He would carry me with him everywhere, and take me to bed with him at night and read me stories, and play games with me all day. But now I am old and dusty. No one will *ever* want me now!"

The bear and the doll had been so busy talking, they hadn't noticed that Mrs. Periwinkle, the owner of the shop, had climbed up on a stepladder just below their shelf. And just at that moment she reached up and lifted down the big porcelain doll. The doll was so startled, she almost squealed.

"Here is the last doll in the toy store," said Mrs. Periwinkle. "It's Christmas Eve and we'll be closing soon. I don't think you'll find another doll in the whole town at this late hour."

"Well, her bow is a little rumpled... and one of the buttons on her shoe is missing," mused a gentle-looking old lady as she held the doll. "But she will just have to do!"

So into a big green box filled with pink tissue paper went the porcelain doll.

She only had a moment to wink one

last farewell to her old friend, the teddy bear, before the lid covered her head. A big ribbon went around the box, and out the door went the bright package, under the arm of the kind old lady who had bought it.

How lonely the teddy bear felt! The shelf seemed so empty now, after all the years he'd shared it with the big porcelain doll. How he would miss her. He glanced at the clock below. The shop should be closing any minute now. "This will be one more Christmas Day I'll spend in the toy shop," he thought to himself.

Mrs. Periwinkle closed the front door and began to turn out the lights. Suddenly there was a great banging at the door and a small voice called, "Let me in, let me in! Oh, please let me in!"

"I'm sorry, but the shop is closed," Mrs. Periwinkle called through the door. "You're too late!"

But when she parted the curtains and saw that it was just a little girl, her heart softened and she opened the door.

"Oh, please!" said the child. "I *must* have a gift for my little brother. He's just come home from the hospital for Christmas!" She looked up. "There! That teddy bear, that's just the thing! Please, may I have it?"

"But it's old and dusty," said Mrs. Periwinkle. "Why not take one of these brand-new trucks? Or look, what about this wooden puppet?"

"No," said the little girl. "My brother would want something soft and cuddly. The teddy bear is just right. I'll buy it...please wrap it up!"

So down came the teddy from the shelf, and into the box he went, and out the door. Oh, what an adventure, after all those quiet years in the toy store. How he smiled when he heard the sleigh bells in the street and the laughter of all the merry people hurrying home on Christmas Eve. Deep inside the dark box his little bear heart beat happily. At last he would have a home, just like all the other teddy bears in the world.

He could hardly wait till morning! After his box had been placed under the Christmas tree, the teddy bear dreamed during the long, silent night of what it would be like to live in that fine home and belong to the little boy. And then, suddenly, before he knew it, there were voices and footsteps and laughter...and it was Christmas morning! And before long, off went the lid of his box, and bright Christmas tree lights lit up the little bear's world.

At first he could hardly see—it was so bright and rainbow-shiny in that cozy room.

But, oh! he could *feel*! He could feel a little boy's arms hugging him tight, and he could hear a little boy's voice say, "Oh, a teddy bear! A teddy bear! Just what I've always wanted, and now he's MINE! My very own teddy bear!"

You might well imagine that that would be the end of this happy story, but there is one question that some child is sure to ask: Did the teddy bear ever see the big porcelain doll again? (And certainly, one would think *not*...for how unlikely it would be that the big doll should ever be taken to that same house out of all the houses in that whole big city.)

But that's exactly what happened. That very day, when the little girl and her baby brother ran to welcome their grandmother as she climbed the front steps for her Christmas visit, what do you think she had in her arms? A bright red fire truck for her grandson...and a big green box for his big sister. And who do you think was in that big green box? It was the porcelain doll, of course, and oh! wasn't the teddy bear happy to see her!

So now, once again, the doll and the bear sometimes sit side by side on a shelf. But now each of them is loved by a special child...and that's the very best thing that can ever happen to a big porcelain doll and a teddy bear!

SANTA'S WORKSHOP

The Christmas Elves are busy
in Santa's cozy shop
fixing up surprises
there is no time to stop

All the little reindeer
are waiting near the sleigh
to carry Santa through the air
and help him on his way

So sleeping children everywhere,
  . . . those happy girls and boys,
may wake on Christmas morning
  to find their share of joys.

A CHRISTMAS

A Angel	**B** Bear	**C** Candy Canes

D Drum	**E** Elf	**F** Fireplace

G Gingerbread Man	**H** Holly	**I** Ice Skates

ALPHABET

J Jingle Bells

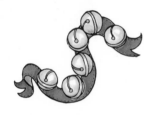

K Kings

L Lamb

M Mouse

NOEL

N Nuts

O Ornament

P Poinsettia

Q Queen

R Reindeer

S Santa Claus

T Tree

U Unicorn

V Violin

W Wreath

X Xylophone

Y Yarn

Z Zebra

Merry may
your Christmas be
In every way
... from A to Z

THE GINGERBREAD FAMILY

Let us bake some ginger men,
Some ginger ladies too,
And some ginger babies.
I'd like some . . .

    Wouldn't you?

You will need:

¼ cup butter, softened	½ teaspoon cinnamon
½ cup brown sugar	1 teaspoon ginger
½ cup dark molasses	¼ teaspoon salt
3½ cups sifted flour	¼ cup water
1 teaspoon baking soda	Cinnamon candies
¼ teaspoon ground cloves	Raisins

Ask a grownup to help you.

Preheat oven to 350 degrees. Cream butter and sugar together with the back of a wooden spoon. Add molasses. Beat well. Sift dry ingredients together and add to butter mixture in 3 parts, alternating with water. Roll dough out on floured board. Cut into gingerbread men shapes with cutter or cardboard pattern. Lay 2 inches apart on cookie sheet and decorate. Place three cinnamon candies down the middle of each gingerbread man to make his buttons. Add one candy to the face to make his nose. Cut one raisin in half for each man to make his eyes, and use another raisin to make his mouth. Bake 8 to 10 minutes. Yield: 10 cookies.

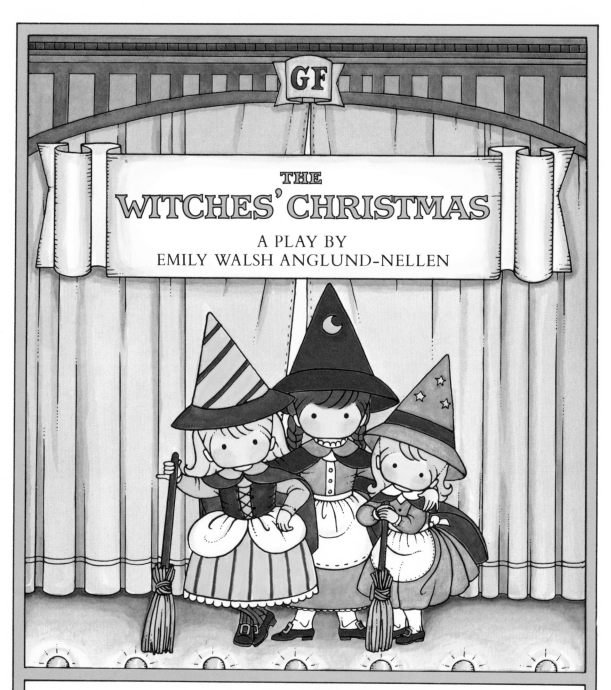

THE WITCHES' CHRISTMAS

A PLAY BY
EMILY WALSH ANGLUND-NELLEN

THE CAST

THREE WITCHES	THREE CHILDREN
TURNIP, the oldest witch	PETER, the oldest child
EFFIE, the middle witch	MARY, the middle child
HILDA, the youngest witch	MICHAEL, the youngest child

Performed December 18, 1980, at 8:36 a.m., Green Farms Academy, on the stage in the big gym

(*The curtain opens. Three witches are sitting in the forest.*)

HILDA: Why are we staying here so long after Halloween?

TURNIP: We're waiting to see what happens. I've been curious all these years.

HILDA: Curious about what?

TURNIP: I've heard that something *special* happens and I want to find out what it is!

EFFIE: While we're waiting, let's trick some people.

HILDA: Yes, I *love* tricking people. That's fun.

TURNIP: Then let's go! (*Curtain*)

(*Witches peek in window and see children putting up a tree.*)

HILDA: What are they doing?

EFFIE: I don't know. Let's listen and maybe we'll find out.

(*The witches hide and listen. The children begin to talk.*)

PETER: Putting up a Christmas tree is hard work. I'll set it up, Mary. You get the ornaments, and we'll have it all ready before Mother gets home from work.

MICHAEL: What do *I* get to do?

MARY: You can come and help me!

MICHAEL: All right. Can I bring Teddy Bear too?

PETER: (*Whispers to Mary*) He should learn to be a man, like *me*. You baby him too much.

MARY: Oh, let him bring his bear. It's Christmas Eve.

PETER: Well, I wish he was older and more helpful. Since Father died, Mother needs all of our help now.

MICHAEL: When are we going to get the decorations?

MARY: Right now! They're outside in the shed.

MICHAEL: I want Christmas to be happy. And I want Mommy to be happy too. I want her to laugh the way she always used to.

MARY: Don't worry, Michael. We're going to be happy this Christmas. You'll see. (*They open the door.*)

TURNIP: Oh! They're coming out here. Quick! Let's hide in these pine trees.

(*Mary and Michael go out to the shed.*)

MARY: You wait out here, Michael, while I get the ornaments. (*She goes inside.*) It's dark in here. (*Michael sees the witches hiding.*)

MICHAEL: Can I come in with you, Mary? I see three people with black hats on. They look like witches!

MARY: (*Calling from inside shed*) Don't be silly, Michael. There are no such things as witches!

MICHAEL: But—but I *see* them! I really do! Three of them! I'm afraid!

MARY: Be quiet, Michael!

PETER: (*Peeks his head out the door and calls*) When are you coming back with the ORN-A-MENTS?

MARY: (*Calling*) I can't find the right box. Come here and help me! (*Peter comes out and sees the witches too.*)

PETER: Mary, there are *real live witches* out here!

MARY: (*Calling*) Nonsense! (*She comes out of the shed slowly.*) You and Michael are imagining things. (*She sees the witches.*) Oh! You really are witches!

TURNIP: Yes! My name is Turnip.

EFFIE: I'm Effie.

HILDA: I'm Hilda.

MICHAEL: You're not supposed to be here now! Halloween is over!

MARY: It's December twenty-fourth, the day before Christmas! What are you doing here?

TURNIP: We want to see what happens on Christmas.

HILDA: What is Christmas anyway?

PETER: Why, it's the happiest day of the year!

MARY: Christmas is the time when people are kind to each other.

MICHAEL: Christmas is tomorrow!

MARY: And that is why we must hurry! There is so much to do. (*Mary, Peter, and Michael start to go inside.*)

25

TURNIP: (*Smiling kindly*) I guess we'll be going, too, now that we know what Christmas is. Good-bye.

MARY, MICHAEL, AND PETER: Good-bye. (*The witches leave.*)

TURNIP: (*Whispering slyly to the other witches*) We'll pretend to go now, but we'll come back and play some tricks on them.

(*The three children go in and begin to decorate the tree.*)

MARY: Oh, this is fun. Let's sing a Christmas song while we work. (*They sing "Deck the Halls with Boughs of Holly." Soon the tree is decorated.*)

MARY: Oh, isn't it lovely!

PETER: Yes, it's going to be a good Christmas.

MICHAEL: (*Yawns*) I'm getting sleepy.

PETER: Now, let's put our presents under the tree.

MARY: And then we'll all go to bed. Mother will be surprised when she gets home to find everything ready and us asleep. (*The children go off-stage and bring back some presents. They put them under the tree.*)

PETER, MARY, AND MICHAEL: (*kneeling to say a prayer near their beds*) God bless everyone in the world, and give peace and happiness to all.

MARY: Good night.

PETER: Good night and Merry Christmas!

MICHAEL: Yes, Merry Christmas! (*He yawns. They go to sleep. Later, the witches sneak into the house.*)

TURNIP: It will be morning soon. What can we do to trick them?

EFFIE: Let's eat these candy canes.

HILDA: Let *me* have one! (*Michael wakes up and sees the witches. One of them starts to eat a candy cane.*)

MICHAEL: You're back! Are you hungry? Would you like some fruit-cake and cookies? (*He gives some to* TURNIP *and* EFFIE.) You see, that's what Christmas is. Christmas is sharing.
(PETER *and* MARY *wake up.*)

MARY: That's right! And Christmas is thinking about others too. Those boxes are presents.

TURNIP: Presents? What are presents?

PETER: When you think someone needs or really wants something special, you save your money to buy it or you make it yourself. You wrap it up carefully so it will be a surprise on Christmas morning. That's what presents are!

EFFIE: Well, I could use a new broom.

HILDA: And I could use a new book of magic spells.

TURNIP: And I certainly could use a new hat.

(*PETER, MARY, and MICHAEL look at each other sadly.*)

PETER: We're sorry but we have none of those things to give you.

TURNIP: That's all right . . . because I think I'm beginning to understand

28

what Christmas means. It isn't the candy canes, or the decorations, or the presents... it's people *caring* about one another that makes Christmas special. It's that Christmas spirit that we'd really like to share with you.

MICHAEL: Then why don't you?

MARY: What are we waiting for?

MICHAEL: Merry Christmas!

PETER: It's Christmas, everyone! It's Christmas!

(*The children and the witches dance in a circle.*)

ALL: (*Singing*) Jingle bells, jingle bells...

EFFIE: You were right—Christmas is the happiest day of the year!

ALL: Merry Christmas and God bless us *all*, each and *every one*!

A VERY SPECIAL DAY

I open my eyes.
I sit up in bed.
The sky is just getting light.
This is a Special Day...
I cannot sleep any longer.

I wake my little brother.
We go down the hall
to Mommy and Daddy's room.
We open the door.
We are very quiet.

Then, suddenly, we laugh out loud
and hop into bed with them!
They are surprised, but they laugh too.
We all snuggle and giggle a while.
Then we put on our robes and slippers
and all go downstairs... together!

30

Suddenly . . . there it is!
Our Christmas Tree!
With all its bright lights
and shiny balls and tinsel.
It is so beautiful!

My brother and I
rush to the fireplace.
We take down
our stockings.

We want to see
what Santa
has brought.

Next we open the boxes
under the tree, one by one.
We tear open the pretty wrappings
and find the surprises hidden inside . . .

a book for me,
a bike for my brother,
a scarf for Mother,
a tie for Daddy.
Even our kitten
gets a toy mouse!

I find a dollhouse.
My brother finds a teddy bear.
There are so many surprises.
Soon the floor is covered
with paper and ribbon.

Mother calls us to the table.
She gives each of us
a special Christmas cake
with red and green fruit inside . . .

and nuts and currants too!
Oh, how good it tastes.
It is so cozy and warm
in our kitchen.

Later we take a walk
in the deep white snow
and feed the birds.

Soon our friends
arrive with packages,
and we run to
the door to welcome
them.

Soon it is time for dinner.
My brother and I
help to carry in the big turkey.

We all say a prayer.
Then we eat turkey
and mashed potatoes...
and we have pumpkin pie
for dessert!

After everyone has gone,
Daddy holds me on his lap
and reads to me from my new book.
Mommy plays the piano
and we all sing songs.

Then the fire is low . . .
we look out our window
and see the stars.
Our Christmas tree, too,
looks like a tree of stars
in the darkness of our cozy room.

We climb the stairs,
and Mother hugs each of us,
and Daddy tucks us in.

I try to stay awake . . .
but soon my eyes close . . .
and I think to myself before I dream,
"What a happy Christmas
this has been!"
It was a Very Special Day!

MEMORIES
OF A
CHRISTMAS TREE

They brought me in from frost and snow
    and dressed me in a rainbow glow.
They filled my arms with lovely things...
    great balls of lights...glass birds with wings.
They wove red berries in my hair
    and candy canes were hidden there.
They dazzled me with garlands, gold,
    and all the trinkets hands could hold.
With joyful songs, the air was sweet,
    and gifts were nestled at my feet.
From every branch burned candles, bright,
    till all my glory filled the night.
Then, young and old, they circled round,
    and like a King, by subjects, crowned,
as Royalty...from lands afar,
    upon my head...they placed
    A STAR!

THE
BEST GIFT OF ALL

Oh! What can we give
    to show that we care?
In every store window
    what trinkets are there!
Oh, there's so much to buy
    upon every store shelf
But the best gift of all
    is the gift of one's self.

A CHRISTMAS STORY

I t was Christmas Eve. The little town was covered with a
fresh dusting of white snow. Everyone was happy and busy
doing last-minute shopping, wrapping last-minute gifts, and
hurrying off to visit friends.

All the houses were decorated with holly wreaths and pine branches. Bright Christmas trees stood in every window, shining with tinsel and rainbow-colored lights. Laughter and merriment were everywhere.

Only one little house was dark and quiet. That house was the home of old Mrs. Plum, who lived all alone on the edge of town. Her husband had died many years before, and all her children had grown and moved away.

Everyone in the town was so busy on this special night, no one even noticed that there was no Christmas tree in her window... there were no holly wreaths decorating her doorway... and there were no Christmas gifts waiting to be opened on Christmas morning.

Mrs. Plum knew there would be no Christmas at all for her, so she told herself she didn't care about Christmas anyway. She decided to go to bed early and sleep until Christmas was over.

But, even though almost everyone else in that busy town had forgotten her, there was one little girl who remembered Mrs. Plum. It was little Jenny, who, one cold blustery winter day a year ago, had gone skating and fallen through the ice.

Jenny remembered that day very well, and she also remembered the kind old lady who had pulled her out of the icy water just in time and had bundled her up in warm blankets and taken her home. After that day Jenny was so ill that she had to stay in bed all winter long.

At first her friends from school had stopped by to visit, but gradually they became too busy with school and other playmates to bother any longer. And one by one they stopped coming to see Jenny until, at last, she was all alone. She had been so lonely waiting in that bed, all by herself, that long year through.

Since Jenny had been so lonely herself, she knew how Mrs. Plum felt. She knew very well that everyone needs some kindness now and then . . . everyone needs a friend to help her through the difficult days. Besides, Jenny didn't think it was right for anyone to miss Christmas. So Jenny made a plan. If Mrs. Plum wouldn't come out to celebrate Christmas, Jenny would bring Christmas in to her.

So Jenny sat down and sewed a cozy shawl out of a nice warm piece of wool she'd saved. Then she baked a little spice cake filled with nuts and currants.

She packed her gifts in a basket and started off toward Mrs. Plum's house.

Along the way she met a boy named Willie. He was new in town. He didn't know any of the children, so nobody played with him very much. Jenny took the time to stop and talk to him, and then she decided to ask him if he'd like to help bring Christmas to someone who needed it.

Willie knew how it felt to be left out and forgotten, and he didn't want anyone else to ever feel that way, so he smiled and said, "Yes, but I have no money or gifts. What can I bring to help make someone's Christmas happy?"

Jenny answered, "I heard you playing your flute the other day, from my window. It sounded so lovely. You don't need anything else. You can bring the gift of song." So Willie hurried home and got his flute, and soon he was walking beside Jenny through the thickening snow.

They hadn't gone far when they came upon a small gray kitten, shivering in the cold.

"Meow," it whispered pitifully. It was Christmas Eve, and no one had stopped to care about a tiny gray kitten lost in the dark. They were much too busy going to parties and having fun. But Jenny and Willie weren't too busy. They stopped and Jenny said, "Let's take this kitten to Mrs. Plum. Then she won't be alone anymore. She'll always have someone to care for."

When they arrived at Mrs. Plum's house, they stood outside her door and began to sing very softly and sweetly. They sang the old treasured carols, which told of Christmases long ago.

After a while the door opened very slowly and Mrs. Plum peeked out to see who could be caroling outside her house. When the children saw her, they shouted, "Merry Christmas, Mrs. Plum. Merry Christmas!" Oh, she was so surprised, and oh, she was so happy that she had been remembered.

"Merry Christmas to you too," she answered. Then she invited them in, and soon they were all having tea in her tiny parlor and sharing the sweet, spicy cake that Jenny had baked. Willie played his flute, Jenny gave Mrs. Plum her presents, and the kitten just hopped up onto Mrs. Plum's lap and purred.

Suddenly and surprisingly, Mrs. Plum chuckled. She hadn't done that in years. So this was what Christmas was like. She'd quite forgotten how lovely and warm and bright and shining it could be.

Then Mrs. Plum decided that she would give a gift, too, this Christmas. She gathered the children in her arms and sat them beside her on the tiny, soft sofa. "Do you children like stories?" she asked.

"Oh, yes!" they shouted.

"Would you like to hear some special Christmas tales from long ago that I've saved up through all these years?"

"Oh, yes!" they both answered and snuggled closer.

Mrs. Plum sat by the fire, and in the hush of that snowy Christmas Eve, to the listening children, she gave *her* Christmas gift . . . the gift of Memories.

"Once upon a time, a long time ago, there was a lovely bright star, and three wise men who followed it . . . searching . . . and in a tiny town called Bethlehem, a Child was born . . ." And on through the quiet night, her gentle voice retold the favorite Christmas tales till the fire burned to glowing embers.

And so it was, on that special Christmas Eve, in that tiny house, in the snow, that each of them gave their gifts to one another. And in such a way, gift by gift, and Christmas by Christmas, the magic continues down through the years.

A CHRISTMAS PRAYER

Upon this Special Day...
We celebrate
the birth
of Christ.

Jesus was born
to bring us Love.

He has put his arms
about us,

...and gathered us to Him,

and
in that loving circle,

there is room
for
All.